Alfred A. Knopf
New York

THE START

KIT FEENY: THE UGLY NECKLACE

Alfred A. Knopf
New York

THIS IS A BORZOI BOOK PUBLISHED BY ALFRED A. KNOPF

Visit us on the Web! www.randomhouse.com/kids

Educators and librarians, for a variety of teaching tools, visit us at www.randomhouse.com/teachers

Library of Congress Cataloging-in-Publication Data
Townsend, Michael (Michael Jay).
Kit Feeny : the ugly necklace / by Michael Townsend. — 1st ed.
p. cm. — (Kit Feeny ; #2)
Summary: Kit Feeny, a young bear, enters into a competition with his sisters to see who can give their mother the best birthday present.
ISBN 978-0-375-85615-0 (trade) — ISBN 978-0-375-95615-7 (lib. bdg.)
1. Graphic novels. [1. Graphic novels. 2. Gifts—Fiction. 3. Family life—Fiction. 4. Bears—Fiction.] I. Title.
PZ7.7.T69Kf 2009
741.5'973—dc22
2008040155

Pen and Ink Drawings With Digital Coloring

MANUFACTURED IN MALAYSIA
October 2009
10 9 8 7 6 5 4 3 2
First Edition

Random House Children's Books supports the First Amendment and celebrates the right to read.

TABLE OF CONTENTS

1. MONKEY SAYS WAKE UP NOW!

2. THE BEST GIFT EVER?

3. FAILURE, FAILURE, FAILURE, AND MORE FAILURE

4. ELVIS, ICE CREAM, AND AN EMPTY HOLE

5. BUNNY LOOKS GOOD, BUT WILL MOM?

6. AND THE WINNER IS . . .

PART 1. MONKEY SAYS WAKE UP NOW!

AS THE SUN ROSE ON A BEAUTIFUL SATURDAY MORNING, THE EVIDENCE OF A WONDERFUL SLEEPOVER SLOWLY CAME TO LIGHT.
INSIDE THE FEENYS' HOUSE...

TWO EXHAUSTED TREASURE HUNTERS SLEPT SOUNDLY...
TWEET
TWEET
TWEET
TWEET

UNTIL THEY WERE AWAKENED BY AN ANGRY DIGITAL MONKEY.
MONKEY SAYS WAKE UP NOW!

MONKEY SAYS WAKE UP NOW!

YAWN
WHAT IS THAT SOUND?
MONKEY SAYS WAKE UP NOW!
IT'S MY NEW ALARM!

MONKEY SAYS WAKE UP OR MONKEY WILL SCREAM!
MY MOM THINKS IT'S ANNOYING.

WHY'S THAT?
MONKEY WARNED YOU! EEEEEK-A EEEEEK-A
WHO KNOWS?

FINALLY FULLY AWAKE, HOFF NOTICED A BAD SMELL.
SNIFF SNIFF
CLICK
WOW, SOMETHING SURE STINKS!
YEP.

YOU'RE SMELLING MY STINKY-SOCK COLLECTION!

ONLY THE STINKIEST OF SOCKS MAKE IT INTO THIS BAG!

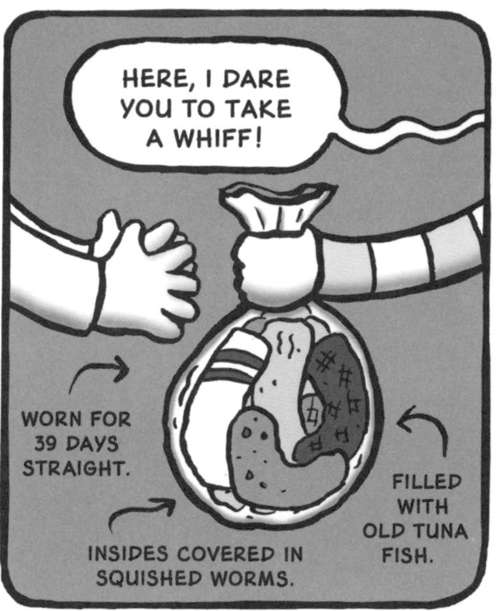
HERE, I DARE YOU TO TAKE A WHIFF!
WORN FOR 39 DAYS STRAIGHT.
INSIDES COVERED IN SQUISHED WORMS.
FILLED WITH OLD TUNA FISH.

SNIFF

?
HACK HACK HACK HACK
HI, DAD!

GOOD MORNING, BOYS!

I'M NOT EVEN GOING TO ASK WHY HOFF WAS SMELLING A BAG OF SOCKS...
OKAY.

BUT I DO WANT TO KNOW WHAT'S WITH ALL THOSE HOLES IN THE BACKYARD?

WE WERE DIGGING FOR TREASURE!

WELL, I HOPE YOU HAVE JUST AS MUCH FUN FILLING THEM BACK IN!

SAY, KIT, DO YOU KNOW WHAT TODAY IS?

UMMM...IS IT NINJA LUMBERJACK AWARENESS DAY?

OR MAYBE IT'S NATIONAL HOFF-IS-AWESOME DAY!

NOPE, I'M SORRY TO SAY IT'S NOT "HOFF-IS-AWESOME DAY" AND I'VE NEVER EVEN HEARD OF NINJA LUMBERJACKS!
WELL, THAT'S BECAUSE THEY'RE SO GOOD...

NOBODY SEES THEM!
GAB GAB GAB
BLAH BLAH

WHOA!
THAT TREE JUST FELL OVER ALL BY ITSELF!
IT MUST HAVE BEEN THE WIND!
SEE, DAD, THAT'S WHY THEY NEED AN AWARENESS DAY!!!

OKAY, BUT IT'S NOT "NINJA LUMBERJACK AWARENESS DAY" EITHER...
THEN WHAT IS IT?

IT'S YOUR MOM'S BIRTHDAY! THE PARTY'S TONIGHT.

KIT WAS SHOCKED TO FIND OUT HE HAD FORGOTTEN HIS MOTHER'S BIRTHDAY AGAIN.
MORNING, GIRLS!
HI, DAD!
EEEP!

HEY, KIT, YOU LOOK LIKE YOU FORGOT TO GET MOMMY A PRESENT AGAIN.
BUT DON'T WORRY 'CAUSE EVEN WHEN YOU REMEMBER, OUR GIFTS ARE STILL SOOOOOOO MUCH BETTER!
ARGGGH!

CHEERS, BONNIE! TO ANOTHER YEAR...
OF US GIVING MOTHER THE BEST GIFT EVER!

YOU TWO BETTER SPIT OUT THAT JUICE BECAUSE...
THIS YEAR, MOM IS GOING TO LOVE MY GIFT THE MOST!

GULP!
YOU WANNA BET?
SURE!
SSIPP

SO, WHAT DO WE GET WHEN WE WIN?
I KNOW! THE LOSER HAS TO WEAR WHATEVER UGLY OUTFIT THE WINNERS PICK OUT!
IN PUBLIC!

DEAL!
DEAL!

HEY, APRIL, SINCE WE ALREADY HAVE OUR GIFT, WHAT DO WE DO NOW?
SSIPP
YOU'RE GONNA LEAVE US ALONE!
OR ELSE!

OR ELSE WHAT?
OR ELSE WE'LL SOCK YOU!

IF YOU PUNCH US, WE'LL TATTLE!
TOTALLY! SIP
NO, NOT THAT KIND OF SOCK!

GROSS
SPEW
THIS KIND!

EEEEEK EEEEEK
HEE HEE
COME, HOFF!
TO MY ROOM. I MUST THINK!

PART 2.

THE BEST GIFT EVER?

A FEW MOMENTS LATER, KIT AND HOFF GOT STRAIGHT TO WORK IN KIT'S BRAINSTORMING HEADQUARTERS.
HEY, KIT, WHAT'S WITH THE HAMMER?

IN ORDER TO CRUSH MY SISTERS, I'M GOING TO BUILD TWO THINKING CAPS...

SMASH

TO HELP US COME UP WITH THE ULTIMATE PRESENT!

SMASH

OKAY, BUT IF I'M GOING TO HELP, I THINK YOU SHOULD FILL ME IN ON SOME OF YOUR PAST GIFTS.

WELL, LET'S SEE...
ONE YEAR, I DID ACTUALLY FORGET, SO I GAVE HER SOME USED COMICS...
HAPPY BIRTHDAY!
UMMM... THANKS.
ELEPHANT GONE CRAZY
BUT EVEN WHEN I DO REMEMBER...

MY **STOOPID** SISTERS PUT THEIR MONEY TOGETHER AND OUTDO ME!

BUT THIS YEAR WILL BE DIFFERENT, BECAUSE WITH MY HELP...
IT'LL BE TWO VERSUS TWO!

TOGETHER WE'LL BE...
UNSTOPPABLE!

THE NEWLY FORMED "CRUSH THE TWINS" TEAM GOT TO WORK.
SCRIBBLE
SCROBBLE
SCRABBLE
SCRIBBLE
SCRUBBLE
SCROOBLE

HERE ARE JUST A FEW OF THEIR BETTER IDEAS:

A NINJA SWORD AND THROWING STAR

-KIT

A METAL DETECTOR

A SHOVEL

A TREASURE MAP

HO

A BABY DRAGON!

-HOFF

HIP HI-TOPS

AND A B-BAL

-KIT

BUT AS KIT LOOKED OVER THEIR IDEAS, HE COULDN'T REALLY IMAGINE HIS MOM ENJOYING ANY OF THEM.
THESE ARE ALL THINGS WE WOULD LIKE, NOT MY MOM!
COULD IT BE THAT THESE THINKING CAPS AREN'T REALLY HELPING?

MAYBE WE NEED SOME BRAIN FOOD INSTEAD!

OKAY, LET'S TRY THAT!
TO THE KITCHEN!

IN THE KITCHEN, KIT NOTICED A VERY LARGE BOX THAT MADE HIM VERY NERVOUS.
HMMMM...LET'S SEE, PEANUT BUTTER, LEMONS, PICKLES, MARSHMALLOWS...
SHOW YOUR LOVE WITH A

SAY, DAD, IS THAT THE GIRLS' GIFT?
YUP.

WOW!
IT'S HUGE!
TOMATOES, JELLY, TINY ONIONS IN A JAR...

YUP.
SHOW YOUR LOVE WITH A
DIAMOND NECK

HEY, DAD! YOU DONE WITH THE NEWSPAPER?

YUP!
THANKS!

LET'S GO, HOFF!

BACK IN THE BRAINSTORMING HEADQUARTERS, KIT SHOWED HOFF HIS BRAND-NEW IDEA!
SO WHAT'S YOUR IDEA?
THIS IS!
LOVE WITH A
DIAMOND NECKLACE
FROM
BARON VON HOBNOB'S
JEWELRY

JEWELRY? MOMS LOVE THAT STUFF!
AND THE STORE IS JUST DOWN THE STREET!

SO YOU WANT TO GET YOUR MOM...
A BIG DIAMOND NECKLACE!
BUT...AREN'T THEY EXPENSIVE?

YOU BET! BUT LOOK.

NO MONEY DOWN FOR ONE YEAR

THAT MEANS WE'LL HAVE ONE WHOLE YEAR TO FIND SOME BURIED TREASURE TO PAY FOR IT!
THAT'LL BE NO PROBLEM!

SO WHILE HOFF BEGAN EATING HIS BRAIN-FOOD SANDWICH...
MUNCH
MONCH
MUNCH
SCRIBBLE
SCRUBBLE
SCRIBBLE
KIT GOT TO WORK DRAWING OUT A DETAILED PLAN TO BUY THE NECKLACE.

THIS IS WHAT HE CAME UP WITH:
TOP SECRET
FOR HANDSOME EYES ONLY!
OPERATION: IMPRESS MOMMY!!!
AND MAKE TWINS CRY!!!
WOW!

STEP 1
DRESS UP REALLY NICE AND TALK ALL FANCY.
WE LOOK SPIFFY!
'TIS TRUE, I SAY.
PIP-PIP!

GO TO STORE AND IMPRESS EVERYONE.
DID YOU REMEMBER TO LOCK UP OUR LIMO?
PIP-PIP!

MY, WHAT SOPHISTICATED RICH MEN.

STEP 2
FIND BIGGEST DIAMOND NECKLACE IN THE STORE.
'TIS THAT THE BIGGEST?
YES, SIR.

STEP 3
GET IT.
'TIS A BIT TINY FOR MY TASTE, BUT I'LL TAKE IT.
VERY GOOD! WILL YOU PAY NOW OR LATER?

OH MY. I LEFT MY WALLET IN MY MANSION.

THEN YOU CAN PAY LATER!

GREAT!
IS THIS FOR YOUR GIRLFRIEND?

GROSS, NO.
'TIS FOR THE BEST MOM EVER.

SHE IS SO LUCKY!

STEP 4
GET OUT.
GOOD DAY, REGULAR PEOPLE.
SEE THOU LATER.
WHAT A PERFECT SON!
I WISH MY STUPID DAUGHTERS WOULD BUY ME A HUGE DIAMOND NECKLACE!

STEP 5
PRESENT MOM WITH GIFT!
HOW WONDERFUL! THIS IS MY BEST GIFT EVER!
GASP!
THE WINNER!

STEP 6
PICK OUT AWESOMELY UGLY OUTFITS FOR THE TWINS.
HMMM... NOT QUITE UGLY ENOUGH!
SOB!
SOB!
SOB!
SANTA

STEP 7
HUNT FOR TREASURE.
I HIT SOMETHING!
OF COURSE!

TREASURE!
BOO-YA!

STEP 8
PAY BACK JEWELRY STORE.
PIP-PIP!
DO YOU ACCEPT TREASURE?
YOU BET I DO!!!

STEP 9
TAKE MY SISTERS TO THE MALL!
MISSION ACCOMPLISHED
THE END

PART 3.
FAILURE, FAILURE, FAILURE, AND MORE FAILURE

A SHORT TIME LATER, KIT AND HOFF ARRIVED AT THE LOCAL THRIFT STORE.
ARE YOU SURE YOU REALLY WANT TO SPEND ALL YOUR MONEY ON CLOTHES?
OF COURSE!
IT'S ALL PART OF MY AWESOME PLAN!

ONCE INSIDE, THEY BEGAN A SERIOUS SEARCH FOR SNAZZY OUTFITS.
YOU WANNA GO KNOCK A FEW BALLS AROUND?
YEE - HAW
CAN I BRING MY HORSE?

DO YOU THINK MY GRANDMA WOULD LIKE THIS SHIRT?
SHE'D LOVE IT! NOW HIT MY HEAD REALLY HARD!
OKAY.
MRS. THRIFT

BOYS!
WORLD'S BEST GRANDMA

THIS IS NOT A PLAYGROUND!

ARE YOU GOING TO BUY ANYTHING OR NOT?

YUP! WE NEED SOME FANCY-PANTS OUTFITS!
PLEASE FOLLOW ME.

WITH MRS. THRIFT'S HELP, THE BOYS QUICKLY FOUND WHAT THEY NEEDED...

AND WERE ON THEIR WAY TO THE JEWELRY STORE.

BARON VON HOBNOB'S
VERY FINE JEWELRY
WOW! THIS PLACE IS FANCY!

UH-OH!
NO CHILDREN WITHOUT SUPERVISION

COME ON, HOFF, WE LOOK EXACTLY LIKE ADULTS!

SO FAR, THE PLAN WAS WORKING PERFECTLY.

DON'T YOU TWO LOOK GOOFY TODAY. ARE YOU GOING TO A COSTUME PARTY?

UM...NO, JUST SHOPPING FOR MY MOM'S BIRTHDAY.
HOW SWEET!

WELL, HAVE AN EXTRA NICE DAY, BOYS!

OH MAN, YOU THINK ANYBODY HEARD HER?
JUST KEEP COOL.

EXCUSE ME, GENTLEMEN?
ARE YOU HERE ALONE?

UM...OF COURSE!
WE LEFT OUR CHILDREN AT HOME WITH OUR GROWN-UP WIVES.

NOW, CAN I VIEWETH YOUR LARGEST DIAMOND NECKLACE?

A LARGE DIAMOND NECKLACE, HUH?

YES, EXTRA SUPER-LARGE!

'TIS FOR MY VERY OLD MOTHER!
EXCELLENT. BUT BEFORE I SHOW YOU ANYTHING, I'M GOING TO NEED TO SEE SOME SORT OF IDENTIFICATION.

UM, SURE...
OOPS...I SEEM TO HAVE MISPLACED MY GIGANTIC WALLET.

BUT IF YOU HAVE A PEN AND PAPER, I'LL PROVE THAT I AM A GROWN-UP!

SCRIBBLE SCRIBBLE
THERE!

THIS JUST SAYS "KIT IS AWESOME."
IN CURSIVE!

AND CURSIVE IS AN ADULT WRITING STYLE. PLUS, DID I MENTION I'VE READ ENTIRE BOOKS WITHOUT PICTURES?

WELL, CLEARLY YOU'RE A GROWN-UP. NOW, HOW ARE YOU PLANNING ON PAYING FOR THIS SUPER-LARGE NECKLACE?

I SHALL USE THE PAY-LATER PLAN!

BUT DON'T WORRY! AS YOU CAN TELL BY MY SPIFFY CLOTHES, I HAVE A HIGH-PAYING JOB.
AND WHAT WOULD THAT BE?

WE'RE TREASURE HUNTERS!

YOU DO ACCEPT TREASURE, RIGHT?

HA HA HA!
DO WE ACCEPT TREASURE?
TEE HEE!
HA HA HA!
GIGGLE! GIGGLE!
IT WAS AT THIS MOMENT KIT REALIZED HIS PLAN WAS NOT WORKING PERFECTLY.

SO, HE DECIDED TO MAKE A QUICK GETAWAY.
PLEASE EXCUSE US.
I THINK I HEARD MY BANKER CALLING!
AND I THINK I LEFT THE WATER RUNNING IN MY HUGE SWIMMING POOL!

HEY, BOYS, MAYBE YOU SHOULD TRY NEXT DOOR AT DISCOUNT SWEETS. THEY HAVE PLENTY OF **CANDY** NECKLACES.

SWEETS
HA HA HA HA HA HA HA HA
I DON'T GET IT. WE WERE SOOO FANCY.
GRRRRR

ARRGGLE
ARGGLE
GGGRR
WACK-A
WACK-A

KIT?
MEWPF!

WHAT AM I GOING TO DO?

GEE, KIT, IT'S NOT THAT BIG OF A DEAL IF YOU LOSE TO YOUR SISTERS.
I KNOW. IT'S JUST THAT MY MOM'S BIRTHDAY PARTY IS IN A FEW HOURS! AND I SPENT ALL MY MONEY ON THESE DUMB CLOTHES!

WHAT WILL MY MOM THINK OF ME? THE SON WHO GOT HER NOTHING?

JUST THEN, THEIR "ALMOST FRIEND" DEVON CAME WALKING DOWN THE STREET.
SNIFF
HEY THERE, WEIRDOS!

GUESS WHERE I'M GOING?
I'M OFF TO HELP WITH THE BIG ANNUAL "CLEAN UP AND SING" DAY IN THE PARK.

OH YEAH, I ALMOST FORGOT THAT WAS TODAY.

I'M GOING TO PUT MY HUGE MANLY MUSCLES TO WORK BY HELPING PLANT SOME TREES!

HEY, PLANTING TREES MEANS DIGGING HOLES!

ARE YOU THINKING WHAT I'M THINKING?
UMMM?

GOOD! LET'S GO TO THE PARK AND DIG!

WHAT'S UP WITH GOOFBALL BOY?
I'LL EXPLAIN ON THE WAY!

PART 4.

ELVIS, ICE CREAM, AND AN EMPTY HOLE

ONCE A YEAR IN THE TOWN OF MACLUNKY, THERE WAS A BIG VOLUNTEER DAY TO BEAUTIFY GENERAL MACLUNKY PARK.
GENERAL MACLUNKY
AND IN CASE YOU ARE WONDERING WHY THERE WERE ELVISES EVERYWHERE...

IT WAS BECAUSE EVERY YEAR AFTER THE CLEANUP, THEY HAD A BIG ELVIS IMPERSONATION CONTEST.
ONE SHOVEL, PLEASE!
IMPERSONATOR SIGN-UP
TICKETS FOR ELVIS UNDER THE STARS
CLEANUP VOLUNTEER SIGN-UP

WOW!
LOOK AT KIT GO!
ACK!
BE PATIENT, TREASURE, I'M COMING!

TREASURE TREASURE TREASURE

WHERE ARE YOU, STUPID TREASURE?

HEY, WORM!
CAN YOU SHOW ME THE TREASURE?

MEANWHILE, ABOVE THE HOLE...
HELLO, BOYS. IT'S SO GOOD TO SEE YOU LENDING A HELPING HAND.
HI, PRINCIPAL KNIGHT!

I'M WARNING YOU, WORM!
HUH?

HEY THERE, KIT!
HAVE YOU MAYBE GONE A LITTLE TOO DEEP?
ACTUALLY, I'M NOT DEEP ENOUGH!
I HAVEN'T FOUND ANY TREASURE YET!

TREASURE?
I NEED IT TO BUY A BIRTHDAY PRESENT FOR MY MOM!

I SEE. YOU KNOW, IT'S PRETTY HOT OUT TODAY. WHY DON'T YOU BOYS LET ME TREAT YOU TO SOME ICE CREAM?

IT'LL COOL YOU DOWN AND YOU'LL BE ABLE TO WORK HARDER!
OKAY!

NOW, MR. WORM, WHEN I GET BACK...

YOU BETTER BE READY TO TALK TREASURE!
UG!

HOWDY-DO, MR. GARTHE! WE'D LIKE SOME ICE CREAM, PLEASE.
CONE OR CUP?

I'D LIKE A CONE WITH... WELL, IT DEPENDS. DO YOU HAVE ANY MONKEY FUDGE?

I ONLY HAVE VANILLA.

YOU MEAN YOU DON'T HAVE ANY BUBBLE GUM?

ONLY VANILLA

PEANUT BUTTER COOKIE CRUNCH?

JUST VANILLA

DOUBLE CHOCO BROWNIE DELIGHT?

VANILLA!

PRETTY SPRINKLE SURPRISE?

I ONLY HAVE VANILLA!

HMMMM... VERY WELL, I'VE ALWAYS WANTED TO COMPETE! I'VE GOT MOVES NO ONE'S EVER SEEN!

SO, KIT, WHAT'S WITH ALL THIS TREASURE TALK?

I'M IN A COMPETITION WITH MY STUPID SISTERS TO SEE WHO CAN GET MY MOTHER THE BEST BIRTHDAY PRESENT. THAT'S WHY I NEED TO FIND SOME TREASURE REAL SOON!
HMMM...
JUST

COMPETITION IS WONDERFUL, AS LONG AS YOU DON'T LOSE SIGHT OF THE MAIN THING.

LIKE WITH TONIGHT'S CONTEST, THE FIRST-PLACE TROPHY WOULD BE GREAT. BUT THE MAIN THING IS THAT I LOVE THE MUSIC!
AND DRESSING UP ALL CRAZY!

WELL, YEAH, THAT TOO!

SO, WHAT IS **YOUR** MAIN...
CRUNCH
THING?
TO GET MY MOM A GREAT GIFT TO...
CRUNCH
SHOW HER HOW MUCH I LOVE HER.

THAT SOUNDS ABOUT...
SLURP
RIGHT!
YEAH, BUT I STILL DON'T HAVE ANY...
SLURP
MONEY!

MAYBE NOT, BUT...
CRUNCH
YOU DO HAVE SOME TALENTS YOU CAN...
CRUNCH
USE TO MAKE A GIFT.
CRUNCH
HMMM...
CRUNCH

HERE, LET ME SHOW YOU SOMETHING.
AHEM!

OH, BABY, B-B-B-B-B-BABY! I LOVE YOU!

WOH-OH OH-OH-OHH HOLD ME TIGHT!

MM MM OH, OH YEAH, YEAH

I'M ALL SHOOK UP!

CLAP CLAP CLAP CLAP CLAP CLAP CLAP CLAP
THANK YOU, THANK YOU VERY MUCH!
WOW!

THAT WAS AWESOME, PRINCIPAL KNIGHT!

I'M GOING TO GO HOME AND MAKE SOMETHING RIGHT NOW!
GOOD LUCK!

MEANWHILE, BACK AT THE "JUST VANILLA" ICE CREAM STAND...
SO, NOW THAT MR. GARTHE'S GONE, WE SHOULD...
MAKE SOME FANTASTIC FLAVORS!

I'LL GO GET US SOME INGREDIENTS!
COOL!
JUST VANILLA

HEY, KIT, I'M GOING THE SAME WAY! WANNA RACE TO OUR STREET?
OKAY!

ELVIS UNDER THE STARS
PIP-PIP-PIP-PIP!
PIP-PIP-PIP-PIP-PIP!
MY, WHAT STRANGE CHILDREN.
ELVIS AGREES.

PART 5.

BUNNY LOOKS GOOD, BUT WILL MOM?

WHEN KIT ARRIVED HOME, HE WAS READY TO BEGIN CREATING SOMETHING AWESOME.
HEY, SON, YOU'RE LOOKING QUITE SPIFFY.
UM...THANKS. SEE YA, DAD!

WAIT, KIT! DID YOU FILL UP THOSE HOLES?
NOT YET.

MAKE SURE IT'S DONE BEFORE YOUR BEDTIME!
SURE THING, DAD.

OH, AND YOUR MOM'S PARTY BEGINS IN 43 MINUTES!
GULP!

ONCE IN HIS ROOM, KIT CHANGED INTO HIS NORMAL CLOTHES...

AND STARTED WORKING.

BLECCH!
MY IDEAS STINK!

THINGS WEREN'T GOING WELL.
GRRRR

KIT FELT DESPERATE.
SO DESPERATE THAT...
HMMM

HE DECIDED TO GIVE HOFF'S BRAIN FOOD SANDWICH A TRY.
EEEEP

MUNCH
CRUNCH CRUNCH

IT DIDN'T HELP.
BLECCH

HI THERE, KIT!
WHAT'S WITH ALL THE GAGGING?
NONE OF YOUR BEESWAX! NOW GET OUT! I'M WORKING HERE.

OH, WE WON'T BOTHER YOU. WE JUST FIGURED SINCE YOU ARE OBVIOUSLY ABOUT TO LOSE...
WE'D PICK OUT YOUR UGLY OUTFIT RIGHT NOW!
!

WOW, CHOOSING JUST ONE THING IS GOING TO BE SO HARD!
HEY, KNOCK IT OFF!

LOOK, BONNIE!
I FOUND THIS UNDER THE BED!
IT'S PERFECT!

KIT HAD ALMOST FORGOTTEN ABOUT THAT SWEATER.

GIVE IT BACK!

IT WAS A CHRISTMAS PRESENT FROM HIS MOM. SHE HAD MADE ONE FOR EACH OF THEM.

THEY'RE SO ADORABLE!

SAY CHEESE!

CLICK

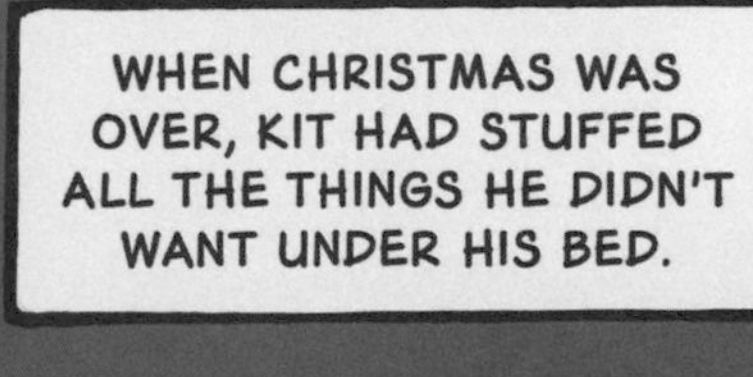

HEY, KIT!
WHAT?

IS THIS ADVERTISEMENT YOUR PRESENT? HEE HEE
SHOW YOUR LOVE WITH A DIAMOND NECKLACE FROM BARON VON HOBNOB'S JEWELRY STORE
OR ARE YOU MAKING A MACARONI RE-CREATION? HA HA

NO AND NO

NOW SCRAM!

SLAM

STUPID TWINS!
JEWELRY STORE

HEYYY, WAIT A SECOND!

THAT'S IT!

EXCITED TO FINALLY HAVE AN IDEA THAT DIDN'T STINK, KIT QUICKLY SET TO WORK.
LOVE WITH A
JEWELRY

AFTER TAKING SOME MEASUREMENTS, HE BEGAN COLLECTING ALL KINDS OF MATERIALS.

SHINY THINGS.

SPARKLY DOODADS.

STICKY GOO.
GLUE

UN-STUFFED FLUFF.
RIIIIPP

ROPES AND CHAINS.

COOL ROCKS.

TOOLS TO PUT IT ALL TOGETHER.

AND A FEW STRANGE GIZMOS.
POLICE

LA-LA-LA!
?
?

SHOULD WE BE WORRIED?

STAND BACK!
GENIUS AT WORK!
SLAM
NAH!
BACK IN HIS ROOM, KIT FEVERISHLY BEGAN...
HAMMERING
SMASH
PAINTING
GLUING
AND TAPPING
TAP
UNTIL FINALLY...

HIS MASTERPIECE WAS...
DONE!

KIT CAREFULLY PLACED THE NECKLACE ON HIS BUNNY, THEN BACKED UP TO TAKE A LOOK.
HOLD STILL, BUNNY.

I LOVE IT!

BUT WILL MY MOM?
DIAMOND NECKLACE
FROM
BARON VON
HOBNOB'S

ACK,
SHE'LL NEVER WEAR THIS!

JUST LIKE I NEVER WORE THAT SWEATER!

KIT,
IT'S TIME FOR YOUR MOTHER'S PARTY!

EEEEP...
IT'S NOT EVEN WRAPPED YET!

THERE.

COMING!

PART 6.

AND THE WINNER IS . . .

BUT TODAY HE WAS A BIT TOO WORRIED TO ENJOY THEM.
GOOD JOB, BONNIE.
VERY CLOSE!

IT'S YOUR TURN, KIT!
OKAY.

THIS IS FROM YOU?
YUP.
PULL IT TIGHTER.
OW!

OH... MY.
SPINNING TIME!
THANK YOU, I GUESS.
SPIN HIM GOOD!
SOB SOB SOB

NOT CLOSE AT ALL!
LOSER!
GIRLS!

HEY, EVERYONE, IT'S CAKE TIME!

YAY!
YAY.

SIGH
WHY ARE YOU EATING SO SLOWLY, KIT?
I BET IT'S BECAUSE HE KNOWS PRESENT TIME IS NEXT!

PRESENT TIME!
WOW! YOUR PRESENT MUST REALLY STINK!
I CAN'T BELIEVE WE WERE WORRIED!

US FIRST!
OKAY!

RIPPPP

HOW WONDERFUL!
A GIANT PHOTO OF MY BEAUTIFUL BABY GIRLS!!!

WHAT DO YOU THINK, MOM?
I LOVE IT! NOW GIVE MOMMY A HUG!

THE MOMENT KIT HAD BEEN DREADING HAD ARRIVED.
INTERESTING WRAPPING, KIT.
THANKS.

GASP!
WOW?
YIPES!

IT'S A NECKLACE, RIGHT?
YEAH.

WE'RE SO GONNA WIN!
HEE HEE HEE

IT...IT HAS SOME FEATURES!
LIKE, IF YOU FLIP THIS SWITCH, IT LIGHTS UP AND MAKES NOISE LIKE A POLICE CAR!

AND IF YOU PULL THIS...
SHWIIIIIP

IT TELLS YOU WHAT ANIMALS SOUND LIKE.
SPIN

A COW GOES MOOO!
HA HA HA
HA HA HA

I'M SOOO SORRY, MOM!
WHY, HONEY?

'CAUSE MY NECKLACE LOOKS NOTHING LIKE A BIG BEAUTIFUL DIAMOND NECKLACE.
TRUE, BUT IT'S SOOO MUCH BETTER.

LOTS OF PEOPLE HAVE DIAMOND NECKLACES. BUT NOBODY HAS A NECKLACE LIKE THIS ONE!
GASP

NOW, WOULD YOU HELP ME PUT IT ON?
SURE.
CLICK

MOM, YOU DON'T REALLY HAVE TO WEAR IT!
BUT I WANT TO! NOW GIVE ME A HUG!

SO, MOM, WHOSE GIFT DID YOU LIKE BETTER?
OH, YOU KNOW I LOVE THEM ALL THE SAME!

HEY, EVERYONE! IT'S TIME FOR MY GIFT!
GOODY!

FIVE TICKETS TO THE "ELVIS UNDER THE STARS" IMPERSONATION CONTEST!
SHWIIIP

NICE GIFT, DAD!

YOU TOO, SON!

KISS

A HORSE GOES NEIGH!

NEIGH NEIGH, APRIL!

MOO MOO, BONNIE!

WHOA, LOOKS LIKE THE CONTEST STARTS REAL SOON!

HMMM...
WELL THEN, WE BETTER GET GOING!

AS THE FEENYS MADE THEIR WAY TO THE PARK, THE GIRLS REALIZED KIT WASN'T WITH THEM.
HEY, WHERE'S OUR GOOFBALL BROTHER?

HERE I AM!

BUT, KIT! THE CONTEST WAS A DRAW!

I KNOW!
?
?

LOOK, MOM!

OH, KIT,
YOU'RE WEARING THE SWEATER I MADE YOU FOR CHRISTMAS! YOU LOOK SOOO CUTE!

BUT, HONEY, IT'S PRETTY HOT OUT! YOU DON'T REALLY NEED TO WEAR IT!

OH, BUT I WANT TO, MOM!
NOW LET'S GO SEE THE SHOW!
YOU BET!

IT HAD BEEN A LONG AND STRESSFUL DAY FOR KIT FEENY, BUT...
HE HADN'T LOST TO HIS SISTERS,
HE LEARNED A LESSON ABOUT GIFT GIVING,
NDER THE STARS
AND HE GOT TO SEE TONS OF GROWN-UPS ACT LIKE TOTAL MORONS!
I'M ALL SHOOK UP!

TO TOP THINGS OFF, HIS PRINCIPAL TOOK FIRST PRIZE!
THE WINNER!
1 #

THAT'S MY PRINCIPAL! I KNOW HIM!
HE GIVES ME TONS OF DETENTIONS!

ONLY MR. GARTHE WASN'T HAPPY WITH THE WAY THINGS TURNED OUT...
YUCK
UH-OH.
ACK
NEW AWESOME MYSTERY FLAVOR -NOT JUST VANILLA

WHAT'S GOING ON HERE?
YOUR NEW "AWESOME MYSTERY FLAVOR" IS DISGUSTING!
YOU SHOULD CALL IT BARF CREAM!

WHAT DID YOU BOYS DO?

WE MADE A NEW FLAVOR.

IT'S...UM... PICKLE-MARSHMALLOW TOAST.

GRRRRRRR.
CAN YOU BOYS RUN FAST?
WHY?

BECAUSE YOU DON'T WANT ME TO CATCH YOU!

EEEEEEEEEEK

GOOD NIGHT, GUYS!
GOOD NIGHT, KIT!

SO, MOM, DID YOU HAVE A GOOD BIRTHDAY?
IT WAS MY BEST BIRTHDAY EVER!

AND NOW IT'S TIME TO GO TO BED!
SO WE CAN HAVE SWEET DREAMS...
ABOUT UNICORNS AND TWIN PRINCESSES!
I HATE SLEEP!

I'M GLAD TO HEAR YOU SAY THAT, KIT, 'CAUSE YOU STILL HAVE SOME HOLES TO FILL IN!
OH YEAH.
HEE HEE

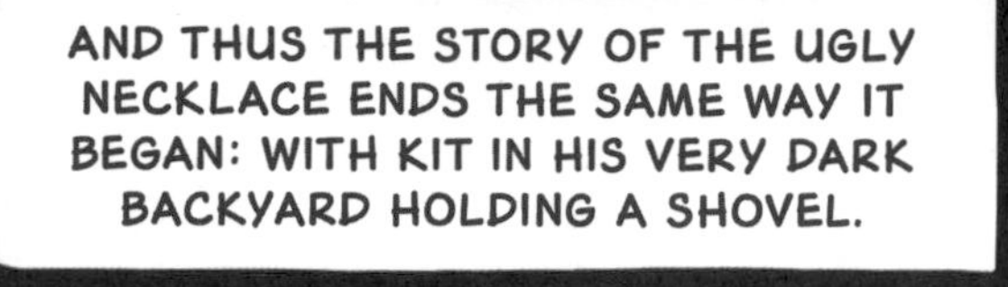
AND THUS THE STORY OF THE UGLY NECKLACE ENDS THE SAME WAY IT BEGAN: WITH KIT IN HIS VERY DARK BACKYARD HOLDING A SHOVEL.
HEY, HOLES, I HOPE YOU'RE HUNGRY!
'CAUSE I'M GOING TO FEED YOU A TON OF DIRT!
OPEN WIDE!

THE

END